W9-BBW-839
YEAR 1972

For Didi who first thought of it
and Shankar who made it possible

The Elephants and the Mice

A Panchatantra Story

Retold and Illustrated by MARILYN HIRSH

THE WORLD PUBLISHING COMPANY
NEW YORK AND CLEVELAND

Library of Congress catalog card number: 70-101838

Printed in the United States of America.

ONCE upon a time in India there was a large city beside a lake. It was a beautiful city. It had many temples and fine houses. The people who lived there were rich and happy. But time passed, and this beautiful city fell into ruins. All the people left it, and they took with them their cows, bullocks, horses, and elephants.

Only the mice who lived in that city stayed on. They began to live in all the old houses and temples. The city beside the lake became a city of mice. Soon there were more mice than there had ever been before. In every family there were grandfathers and grandmothers, fathers and mothers, husbands and wives, uncles and aunts, brothers and sisters and cousins, and lots and lots of baby mice.

All these families of mice lived happily together. They were always having feasts and festivals. There were spring festivals and harvest festivals, and many other festivals. Then there were weddings and all kinds of parties. Nearly every day the mice had some kind of a feast.

In a jungle far from this city of mice there lived some elephants. They were a large herd and their king was a great noble tusker. He was wise and kind and he ruled his herd well. All the elephants loved him and were always loyal to him. The elephants were happy in the jungle, but there came a time of great trouble. There was no rain for several years and all the rivers and tanks dried up. The elephants had no water to drink. The great noble tusker, the king, sent his elephants far and wide in search of water. Finally he learned that on the other side of the ruined city was a large lake.

With great joy the king led all his elephants to the lake. They went as quickly as they could, for they were very thirsty. On the way to the lake the elephants passed right through the ruined city. As the great elephants rushed along they did not notice that the homes of thousands of tiny mice were being crushed beneath their feet. More and more elephants passed through the city of mice.

The mice were in great sorrow. Many mice were homeless and some of the others were hurt. Those who needed help were looked after by the mouse doctors and nurses.

Then at last the dry spell ended, and the elephants were ready to leave the lake and go back to the jungle again. They would be coming through the old city once more! The mice called a meeting. Such a terrible thing had never happened to them before. They must find a way to stop the elephants from harming them. What could they do?

They talked and talked, and then one wise old mouse said he thought they should go to the elephant king and tell him what had happened. And they should ask the elephants to agree not to pass through their city again.

All the mice agreed to this. They chose three very brave mice and sent them to the elephant king. The three mice bowed to the elephant and said, "O great king, you are big and powerful. But when you and your elephants passed through the ruined city you did great harm to us. We are small, and you crushed our homes beneath your feet. Thousands of us were left homeless and many were injured.

"We fear that if you pass through our city again none of us will be left alive. So we have come to ask you if you would kindly go back to your jungle by some other way. If you do that we shall always be grateful to you and we shall be your friends. And even though we are small, perhaps one day we may be able to help you."

The elephant king thought over all that the three mice had said. "Yes, you are right," he said. "We will find some other path to our jungle. Go back to your city and live in peace."

Not many years later, the king of a nearby country needed more elephants for his army. He sent his men into the jungle to catch as many elephants as they could.

The king's men went to the jungle where the elephant king lived. They were happy to find such a large herd of elephants. They dug many deep pits in the jungle and covered them over with branches and leaves cut from the trees. They did this so that when the elephants walked over the branches and leaves they would fall into the pits.

The elephant king and many of his herd fell into the pits. They were trapped. They tried and tried, but they could not get out. Then the men came back and brought with them some tame elephants. With strong ropes the tame elephants pulled all the other elephants out of the pits, and the men took the ropes and firmly tied the captured elephants to big trees.

The men then went back to tell the king what they had done. They took the tame elephants with them.

All the elephants that had been caught and tied to the trees felt very unhappy. The elephant king was sad to see that so many of his herd had been caught. How could they escape? He tried and tried to think of a way to get free, but he could not think of any way.

Suddenly he remembered the mice in the ruined city. Those mice had said they would help him.

The elephant king called his queen. She had not fallen into a pit, so she was free. He asked her to rush to the city of mice and tell them what had happened.

The elephant queen hurried away. When she reached the city she called softly to the mice and told them how the elephants had been caught. The mice were very sorry to hear that the elephants were in such great trouble. They said at once that they would do their best to help their friends.

Then thousands and thousands of mice rushed to the jungle where the elephants were tied to the trees. Many mice went to each elephant and with their strong teeth they cut through the ropes. The elephants were free! The elephants and all the mice were very happy. The king and queen of the elephants thanked the mice for setting them free so cleverly. One mouse sat on the trunk of the elephant king. "We are your friends," he said. "We are glad that we could help you."

The mice and the elephants all sat down together to a great feast. "This is the happiest festival of all," said the mice. "It is a festival of friendship between mice and elephants."

And from that day the mice and the elephants were close friends and they all lived happily ever after.

About the Story

The Panchatantra (or Five Books) is a collection of hundreds of tales. They were first gathered and written in the Sanskrit language over two thousand years ago in Kashmir. From there the tales have spread all over the world. La Fontaine used the Panchatantra stories as a source for some of his fables. In India nearly every child is familiar with the tales, which teach wise (and often shrewd) conduct. Because the stories are familiar all over India, this particular adaptation has purposely not been set in any one locality. The architecture is from Mahabalipuram in the south. The costumes are northern, mainly Rajastani in style. The customs and ceremonies are Maharashtri or Gujarati, from the western part of India.

The Elephants and the Mice comes from the Panchatantra book that is called "The Winning of Friends." Therefore an appropriate ceremony is shown on the dedication page—the elephants and the mice tying rakis (little colored pompoms) on one another. This ceremony is performed once a year on its own holiday. If you tie a raki on someone he must be your faithful friend and must protect you for the whole year.